The New York Times Best-Selling Series by
Henry Winkler & Lin Oliver

How to Hug an Elephant

ILLUSTRATED BY SCOTT GARRETT

Grosset & Dunlap
An Imprint of Penguin Random House

For Frank Dines, a man who defines friendship.
And to Stacey, always—HW

For Paula and Mark Waxman,
and the elephants we saw together—LO

For the Furmstons, Mark, Michelle,
Betty, Daisy and Ren—SG

GROSSET & DUNLAP
Penguin Young Readers Group
An Imprint of Penguin Random House LLC

If you purchased this book without a cover, you should be
aware that this book is stolen property. It was reported as "unsold
and destroyed" to the publisher, and neither the author nor the
publisher has received any payment for this "stripped book."

Penguin supports copyright. Copyright fuels creativity, encourages
diverse voices, promotes free speech, and creates a vibrant culture.
Thank you for buying an authorized edition of this book and for complying
with copyright laws by not reproducing, scanning, or distributing any part
of it in any form without permission. You are supporting writers and
allowing Penguin to continue to publish books for every reader.

The publisher does not have any control over and does not assume
any responsibility for author or third-party websites or their content.

Text copyright © 2015 by Henry Winkler and Lin Oliver
Productions, Inc. Illustrations copyright © 2015 by Scott Garrett.
All rights reserved. Published by Grosset & Dunlap, an imprint of
Penguin Random House LLC, 345 Hudson Street, New York,
New York 10014. GROSSET & DUNLAP is a trademark of
Penguin Random House LLC. Printed in the USA.

Typeset in Dyslexie Font B.V.
Dyslexie Font B.V. was designed by Christian Boer.

Library of Congress Cataloging-in-Publication Data is available.

ISBN 978-0-448-48656-7 (pbk)   10 9 8 7 6 5 4 3 2 1
ISBN 978-0-448-48657-4 (hc)   10 9 8 7 6 5 4 3 2

The books in the Here's Hank series are designed using the font Dyslexie. A Dutch graphic designer and dyslexic, Christian Boer, developed the font specifically for dyslexic readers. It's designed to make letters more distinct from one another and to keep them tied down, so to speak, so that the readers are less likely to flip them in their minds. The letters in the font are also spaced wide apart to make reading them easier.

Dyslexie has characteristics that make it easier for people with dyslexia to distinguish (and not jumble, invert, or flip) individual letters, such as: heavier bottoms (b, d), larger than normal openings (c, e), and longer ascenders and descenders (f, h, p).

This fun-looking font will help all kids—not just those who are dyslexic—read faster, more easily, and with fewer errors. If you want to know more about the Dyslexie font, please visit the site www.dyslexiefont.com.

CHAPTER 1

"We're off to the zoo," Ms. Flowers said as the doors of the yellow school bus closed.

Everyone cheered. Our whole class had been looking forward to this field trip all week. My best friends, Frankie and Ashley, were sitting in the seat in front of me. I had the bad luck to have gotten Nick McKelty as my partner. That meant I had to sit next to him on the bus. And that meant I had very little seat. Nick the Tick's thick body took up most of it. I don't mean to gross you out, but my right butt cheek was riding in the air.

"What do you most want to see at the zoo?" Ms. Flowers asked as she walked up and down the aisle collecting our lunches. One of the parents, Ms. Shimozato, held the big yellow container where our lunches would be kept until it was time to eat.

"A giant squid," Luke Whitman said, handing her his brown bag with a salami grease mark covering the bottom.

"We're going to the zoo, Luke, not the aquarium," Ms. Flowers answered. Her voice sounded like she was holding her nose, even though she wasn't. That happens a lot around Luke. "What about you, Hank?"

"I want to see a giraffe tongue," I said. "I hear they're purple and covered in hair."

"So are you, Zipper Fang," Nick said. He threw his arms up in the air and burst out laughing at his usual not-funny joke. That one movement put my nose right next to his armpit, which is not a place any nose wants to be. It smelled like rotten eggs on toast.

"Giraffe tongues are dark in color to protect them from getting sunburned," Ms. Flowers said. "Their tongues are out a lot when they're picking leaves off trees."

That set off a lot of conversation about weird-but-true animal facts. It seemed like everyone on the bus knew one. It was a fun way to spend the bus ride.

"Spiders have eight legs and forty-eight knees," Katie Sperling said.

"Kangaroos cannot walk backward," Frankie chimed in.

"Tigers have striped skin, not just striped fur," Ryan Shimozato said. His mom smiled proudly, as if she had said it herself.

"Elephants are the only animals that can't jump," Ashley said. "That's because they can weigh up to fifteen thousand pounds. Hard to get that off the ground."

"I love them, anyway," I said to Ashley. "I've watched lots of shows about them on television. I hope we get to see one today."

"Well, Hank, I think you're going to get your wish," Ms. Flowers said. "There is an elephant enclosure at the zoo."

"Can we go there first?" I begged.

"We have a tour guide who has the whole morning planned for us,"

Ms. Flowers said. "It's important that we all stay together. Remember our most important rule—no wandering away. And that goes especially for you, Hank."

She didn't even have to say why. I knew what she meant. I get lost a lot. Maybe it's because I still can't tell my left from my right. Last week, Ms. Flowers gave me the attendance sheet to take to the office. She said to walk to the end of the hall and turn right, then go to the water fountain and turn left. I thought I followed her directions perfectly. That is, until I pulled the door open and walked right into the girls' bathroom. Lucky for me, it was empty.

"The zoo is very large,"
Ms. Flowers explained as we pulled
into the parking lot. "You are each
responsible to always know where
your partner is."

After we entered the zoo, we
met our tour guide, Gina, who
told us our first stop was Gorilla
World. While she was telling us all
about what we were going to see,
I noticed Nick wandering away. He
was heading for a cart that sold
toy zoo animals. Since he was my
partner, it was my responsibility
to tell him to stay with the group.
His back was to me, so I couldn't
see what he was doing. I snuck over
to him and whispered in his ear,

so Ms. Flowers couldn't hear.

"You're not supposed to be here," I said.

Suddenly, he wheeled around and flashed what looked like a rat in front of my face. Before I could do anything, he dropped it down the front of my shirt. It felt cold and sticky.

"Aarrgh!" I screamed, before I could stop myself. I pulled my shirt out of my pants, and the sticky thing fell out the bottom of my shirt to the ground. I looked down and saw it was just a rubber rat. I turned around to tell McKelty how annoying that was, but he had already snuck back to the group. So I stood there alone, with everyone in the class laughing at me. Everyone but Ms. Flowers. She did not look happy.

"Hank," she said. "What was the last thing I said to you on the bus? No wandering away."

"But Ms. Flowers, I was just trying to be responsible."

"Well, you didn't succeed, Hank. Now please apologize to Gina for interrupting her introduction to Gorilla World."

I apologized, but it wasn't fair. It was McKelty who had wandered away. I had only gone after him to help. We started down the path that led to the gorillas.

"I'm going to have a fun day with you, Zipperbutt," McKelty said. "You're my favorite kind of partner. You make the animals in this zoo seem smart."

I looked at Frankie and Ashley, who were at the front of the line asking Gina lots of questions. They seemed really happy. Then I looked at Nick McKelty next to me, who snickered just before he tripped me.

"Watch your step," the big creep said.

Only one thought was running through my mind: *Why did I get stuck with this guy?*

CHAPTER 2

Gorilla World was really cool. We walked along a path next to the rain forest the zoo had built to house about twenty gorillas. When we stopped, Gina told us all about them. It was hard to listen to what she was saying, because I was waiting to see the gorillas swing from tree to tree. They just sat on the ground picking bugs out of one another's hair.

I raised my hand.

"When are they going to swing from the branches?" I asked Gina.

"As soon as you show them how, Zipperhead," McKelty mumbled.

"Actually, that's an excellent question," Gina said.

I smiled inside myself. *Take that, McKelty!*

"Gorillas spend most of their time on the ground," Gina explained. "They climb trees only to find fruit."

"I'd climb a tree for a peach," I said, "but definitely not for a plum. They're so sour they make my lips pucker."

Everyone in the class laughed, including Ms. Flowers and Ms. Shimozato.

We stayed in Gorilla World for half an hour, but it seemed like a month to me. Even though gorillas are very interesting, I couldn't wait to get to the elephants. Besides, there's only so long you can watch large apes pick bugs off one another without starting to itch yourself.

Our next stop was the snack bar. Ms. Flowers ordered twenty-one frozen lemonades with the money our parents had sent.

"Frozen lemonades are stupid," Nick complained. "They wrinkle your tongue."

"Then you don't have to get one," Ms. Shimozato said.

"Good. I'll have a double order of cheese garlic fries instead."

That's just what McKelty needed—as if his breath didn't smell bad enough already.

"I'm sorry, Nick," Ms. Flowers said. "We're all getting the same thing. It's frozen lemonade or nothing."

"Fine, while these guys are freezing their tongues off, I'm going to the bathroom."

"That's odd," Ms. Flowers

said. "I don't think I heard you ask permission."

"I did," he lied. "I just did it silently."

"All right, Nick. You have permission to go to the restroom, but your partner has to go with you. And don't be long."

Boy, did I feel sorry for his partner. Then I realized it was me.

"Wait a minute. Does that mean I don't get frozen lemonade?" I asked.

"Of course you will, Hank," Ms. Flowers answered. "We'll have yours waiting when you get back."

Gina gave us directions to the bathroom. It wasn't far away, but there were several left and right turns we had to make. This was the one and only time I was ever happy to be with Nick the Tick. He may be a jerk, but he's a jerk who's better at directions than I am.

On the way into the bathroom, we passed a dad carrying a baby in a backpack. That little kid was lucky . . . he could just ride around on his dad's back and pee in his diapers anytime he wanted. I stopped to give him a high five, but McKelty yanked me away.

"Babies are gross," he snarled at me. "Besides, I want to get back to that frozen lemonade. I'm so thirsty I might drink yours, too."

When the baby heard McKelty's grumpy voice, he burst out crying.

"That's the right call, little guy," I whispered to him.

Inside, the bathroom wasn't crowded. In fact, we were the only ones in there. As usual, McKelty thought he was the boss of me.

"I'll take this stall," he said. "You go to the one on the end."

"Why?"

"Because I need to be alone. And don't even ask why."

That was fine with me. Any plan that puts space between me and McKelty is a good plan.

When I came out of the stall, I washed my hands and waited for him at the sink. I waited and waited. At last, I called out.

"Hey, McKelty. You stay in there any longer and you're going to have to pay rent."

There was no answer.

I walked over to the stall, bent down, and looked to see if I could see his shoes. There was nothing there. With one finger, I pushed open the door. Not only was it unlocked, the stall was empty.

Nick the Tick had struck again. He had ditched me.

I started to panic a little, but then I told myself that I could handle this. I would find my way back all by myself. I just needed to give the situation the old Hank Zipzer attitude.

I took a deep breath and walked out of the bathroom. I looked in both directions. I had absolutely no idea where I was.

the trails had a snack bar on it.

I ask you, why do there have to be so many snack bars at one zoo? How many snacks does a person need?

I stood there and took a deep breath. My mom always says that taking a deep breath will let your brain work better. And sure enough, a great thought jumped into my mind. Maybe I can't read a map. And maybe I don't know left from right. But I can speak English, and so could everyone else in the zoo. All I had to do was find an adult and ask them to take me to the snack bar closest to the gorillas.

That was one great idea, if

I do say so myself. I actually reached my hand over my shoulder and patted myself on the back.

I looked around for a friendly face, and decided to ask a friendly-looking couple who both had cameras around their necks.

"Excuse me," I said, using my best manners. "Do you think you could show me the way to the gorillas?"

They looked at each other and shrugged.

"*Je ne parle pas anglais*," said the man.

"Huh?" I said.

He repeated something that sounded even more foreign. How could it be? Of all the visitors to the zoo, I picked the two who don't speak a word of English.

"*Gracias*, anyway," I said. I didn't think they were speaking Spanish, but I thought I'd throw that out there to impress them.

They shrugged again and walked away. I stood there, trying to figure out what to do next. The only idea that came to me was that I might never leave the zoo. And I wasn't exactly thrilled about spending the night with a bunch of roaring lions close by.

I felt a hand on my shoulder

and spun around, hoping it was Ms. Flowers. It wasn't. It was a woman wearing a brown uniform with a *Wild About Gingerbread* T-shirt.

"I like gingerbread, too," I said to her, "but I have to say I'm not wild about it."

"I don't understand," she said. "Why are we talking about gingerbread?"

"Because that's what it says on your shirt—*Wild About Gingerbread*."

She looked down at her shirt, then back at me, then burst out laughing.

"It says *Wild About Giraffes*," she said. "Not gingerbread."

"At least I was close," I said. "They both start with a G. I'm not much of a reader."

"I wasn't at your age, either," she said, still smiling. "But it didn't stop me from doing something I love. I'm Nora Bicks," she went on. "I work here at the zoo with the giraffes and the elephants. You seem to be lost."

"I'm only half lost," I said. "The half that can't find the snack bar where my class is waiting."

"Is it the one near the gorillas? With the great frozen lemonades?"

"That's exactly the one!"

"I can take you there. I just have to make a quick stop at the elephant enclosure and then check on Elsie."

"Oh, is Elsie your mom?"

"Actually, Elsie *is* my mom's name. That's why I named our newest elephant after her. Elephant Elsie just arrived at the zoo yesterday. We're keeping her separated from the others until we know she's comfortable here at her new home. Come on. We'll say hi, and I'll get you back to your class."

As we followed the yellow line along the path, I couldn't believe that I was actually going to see a real live elephant up close. I couldn't stop smiling.

"If I had a T-shirt," I told Nora, "mine would say *Wild About Elephants*. I think they're very smart."

"They are," she said. "That's one of the reasons why it makes me so angry when they're mistreated. Elsie was in a circus where she wasn't taken care of properly. We rescued her."

By then, we had reached the elephant enclosure. In the distance, I could see three very big elephants standing around a

pool of water, spraying their backs
with their trunks. Next to them,
in a separate fenced-off area, was
another elephant that was rubbing
her body against a tree trunk.

"There's my Elsie," Nora said. "Looks like she's got an itchy back."

"Maybe I could lend her my bamboo back scratcher that I bought in Chinatown," I offered. "It really works. Of course, her back is a lot bigger than mine."

"You wait here," Nora said. "I'm going to run inside and refresh her water. Then I'll take you to the snack bar. It's just up the red trail. You can see it from here."

"Oh, that's okay," I said to Nora. "I can get there from here. It's easy. I'll just follow the red line."

"You sure?"

"Totally sure."

"Okay, Mr. Wild About Elephants," she said. "Nice talking to you."

I watched Nora unlock the gate and walk into the enclosure. Elsie trumpeted when she came in. Nora talked softly to her as she picked up the hose and filled up Elsie's gigantic water bucket. Then Nora opened the gate and went into the enclosure where the other elephants were still spraying each other.

I tried to leave, I really did. I even turned around and walked over to the red trail. But I couldn't do it. I was so close to a real live elephant—one that was probably lonely and scared in her

new home. Poor Elsie. Maybe
she needed a visitor. And maybe
I was that visitor.

Before I could stop myself,
I went to the unlocked gate and
pushed it open.

In a few steps, I was face-to-
face with the largest animal
I have ever seen.

CHAPTER 4

THE FIRST FIVE THINGS I SAW IN THE ELEPHANT ENCLOSURE

BY HANK ZIPZER

1. Elephant poop the size of a house.

2. More elephant poop.

3. Whoops, here comes another one.

4. I better get out of the way or you won't be able to see me.

5. Sorry there's no number five, but when an elephant's got to go, it's got to go!

CHAPTER 5

I just stood there staring into Elsie's big brown eyes, which were about a mile above my head. She stared right back at me. Neither of us moved a muscle. When I have a stare-down with my sister, Emily, she bursts out laughing in about two seconds, so I always win. But Elsie didn't even bat an eyelash.

I wasn't sure whether our stare-down was a good thing or a bad thing. It was definitely good that she wasn't charging at me with her giant tusks. But maybe she was thinking about doing it, which would definitely be bad.

"Hi, Elsie," I whispered. "My name is Hank. Well, really it's Henry, but everyone calls me Hank, so you can, too."

Suddenly, her ears started to flap. In fact, they flapped so hard that I could feel the air brush across my face. I jumped back a few feet. I hoped this was her way of saying, "Nice to meet you, too." But it was possible this was her way of saying, "This is my space, buddy. Now beat it."

Suddenly, I heard footsteps crunching on the leaves of the enclosure. I was pretty sure it was

Nora, coming back from visiting the other elephants.

I knew the right thing to do was to tell Nora I was there. But sometimes the right thing to do isn't always the most fun thing to do. Without thinking, I ducked into the cave that was part of Elsie's enclosure. I hid behind a rock and peeked out. Nora had stopped and was petting Elsie's trunk.

"How you doing, girl?" she said softly.

At the sound of Nora's voice, Elsie started flapping her ears again.

"I know you're happy when your ears flap," Nora said. "I'm glad you're feeling better. That circus you were with didn't take good care of you, but we will."

I was so curious about what happened to Elsie at that circus, but I was hiding so I couldn't ask.

"Do you want a treat?"

She reached into her pocket and pulled out an entire ear of corn. Elsie lifted her trunk and gently took the corn from Nora. Then she popped the whole thing in her mouth. Even from where I was, I could hear her teeth grinding.

I could tell Elsie loved that treat, because her ears starting flapping like crazy. I smiled, thinking about when I have a black and white cookie, which is *my* favorite treat. My ears are too small to flap, but I sure hop around a lot.

"There's more where that came from," Nora told Elsie. "You be a good girl now."

I watched as Nora walked across the enclosure to the high metal fence. She opened the gate, and without looking back, locked it behind her.

Wow, I thought. *This is great. Now it's just me and Elsie!*

The next thought I had was, *Wow. This is not so great. I'm locked in here with fifteen thousand pounds of elephant!*

When Nora was out of sight, I crept out from behind the rock. I thought I was being quiet, but Elsie's big ears obviously worked very well. She whipped around, swishing her tail back and forth. When she saw me, she raised her giant trunk and let out a loud trumpeting sound.

I stood completely still, as if I had turned into a clay statue. Elsie took a step toward me. Then another step. My heart started to beat really fast, and when I say fast, I mean like a speeding race car. What was

Elsie going to do to me? Push me? Sit on me? Crush me?

Breathe, Hank. Don't panic. It's only the largest land mammal on Earth. You can think of something. Look around and use your brain.

My eyes darted around the enclosure, hoping to find an ear of corn that I could give Elsie. That would at least distract her for a minute. Then, I spotted a dusty soccer ball. *Maybe Elsie plays soccer,* I thought. And maybe she was in the mood for a game. You never know.

"Elsie," I said, in my calmest voice. The one I use when I'm trying to explain to my dad why my report card is always so bad. "I'm going to walk over to that soccer ball, and you're going to stay right there. Okay?"

Elsie lifted her trunk and let out another loud trumpet.

"I'm going to take that as a yes," I said. "And here I go."

My brain told my feet to move. At first, they didn't. But then they did. Never taking my eyes off Elsie, I starting creeping toward the ball.

"So Elsie, want to hear a joke?" I asked. "Jokes always make me feel happy. Here it is. What's the best time to go to the dentist? Give up? *Tooth-hurty*."

Elsie didn't move a muscle. I guess she didn't get the joke. That made sense. I mean, elephants don't spend a lot of time in the dentist's chair.

Elsie watched carefully as I took the last few steps toward the ball.

"I'm going to pass the ball to you, very gently," I explained. "And then you pass the ball back to me, very, very, very gently. We humans call that playing soccer."

Keeping my eyes glued to her eyes, I kicked the ball in her direction. When it stopped at her feet, she tilted her big head and just stared at it.

Hank, you dummy! Of course

she's just staring at it. Elephants
don't play soccer.

Suddenly, Elsie lifted her big
round foot and kicked the ball. I
mean, she kicked it right back to
me.

"No! You didn't!" I said,
trapping the ball under my foot.
"That was a perfect pass."

I used the side of my foot to
pass it back
to her. She
looked down
at the ball
again, took aim,
and sent it flying
back to me.

I couldn't
believe it.

I was playing soccer with an elephant. I couldn't wait to tell Frankie and Ashley. I might be the only kid in New York City who had ever done that. In fact, I might be the only kid on the planet.

"Here you go, girl," I said. "Here comes the Zipzer speedball."

I kicked a strong shot in her direction and watched it roll quickly across the dirt. Elsie pulled her foot back and instead of stopping the ball, let loose a speedball of her own. Her huge foot made solid contact with the soccer ball. It took off like a rocket ship, with the dust flying off it like smoke.

And it was coming straight at my head.

CHAPTER 6

The soccer ball was coming at me so fast that it didn't even look like a ball. It looked like those pictures of meteors I've seen hurtling toward Earth—except at that moment, *I* was Earth. I had no time to think. Luckily, my reflexes took over, and I dove into the dirt. When I lifted my head, I saw the ball crash into the fence behind me. It landed so hard, it actually made the chain-link fence rattle.

"You got one hot foot there,

Elsie," I told her. "You should consider going pro."

As I stood up and started to brush myself off, I heard someone calling my name. I've heard that same voice ever since I was two years old.

"Hank!" Frankie called. "Yo, Hank! Where are you?"

"If you can hear us, give us a sign," Ashley yelled.

"I'm in here, guys," I answered.

"Hank," another voice called. "This is Ms. Shimozato. Where exactly are you? We're all so worried."

"I'm in the elephant enclosure. With Elsie."

There was a long silence. Then

Ms. Shimozato said, "You mean you're inside there?"

"As in, actually inside?" Frankie called out.

"As in, next to an elephant?" Ashley added.

"Her name is Elsie," I called out. "Come around the corner to the gate and I'll introduce you."

I looked over at Elsie who was shifting her weight from one foot to the other.

"You're going to meet my best friends," I explained to her. "And Ms. Shimozato. Her son Ryan is in my class."

Elsie didn't seem too interested. She reached out with her trunk and sucked up some dirt from the ground, then sprayed it all over her back.

"Don't be nervous," I said. "You're going to like them as much as you like me."

Two seconds later, Frankie, Ashley, and Ms. Shimozato appeared at the fence. When they saw me inside, standing next to Elsie, Ms. Shimozato let out a shriek.

"Hank, get out of there right this second," she said.

"What's the rush?" I said. "It's safe in here."

"Hank," Ashley said. "In case you haven't noticed, there's a giant elephant standing right next to you."

"Don't worry. Elsie and I are friends. Well, maybe not friends, but teammates."

"Mrs. Flowers sent us to bring you back immediately," Ms. Shimozato said.

"You better listen this time, Zip," Frankie said. "You're in big trouble."

"When you didn't come back with McKelty, Ms. Flowers got

worried," Ashley went on. "She called the office and got a bunch of staff members to help look for you. I talked her into letting Frankie and me go on a search if we promised to stick with Ms. Shimozato and come back right away."

"I can't get out of here," I told them. "The fence is too high, and the gate is locked."

"So you're stuck in there forever?" Ashley asked.

"A zookeeper named Nora has the key," I explained. "She's wearing a T-shirt that says *Wild About Giraffes*. If you find her, she'll help."

"We're on it," Frankie said.

"Hank, you stay right there," Ms. Shimozato told me.

"As if I have any choice," I muttered.

"Come on, children," I heard Ms. Shimozato said. "This is an emergency. We have to hurry."

The three of them ran off down the path and I turned around to see what Elsie was up to. She had wandered over to her cave, where several large bales of hay were stacked up against the wall. She lifted the top one with her trunk and carried it over to the middle of her enclosure.

"You must be hungry," I said to her. "That's a lot of hay for lunch. Talking about lunch, I'm hungry, too. I wish I liked hay, but I'm more of a hot dog guy myself."

Elsie went over to the stack, lifted another huge bale of hay, and brought it back to the middle of her space. Then she picked it up as high as she could and slammed it against the first one. I think she was trying to break them up so she could start eating the hay. Boy, was she strong.

"I bet your trunk could lift me," I said to Elsie. "I weigh a lot less than those bales."

Wait a minute, Hank Zipper brain, I thought. *You may have a hard time in school, but sometimes that brain of yours comes up with a brilliant idea. And this is one of those times.*

"Elsie," I began. "I need your help."

She stopped eating her hay and stared at me.

"That's good," I said. "Now watch me. I'm going to explain what I need you to do. You're going to pretend that I'm a bale of hay, and lift me up and over the fence with your trunk.

Do you think you can do that?"

Elsie just kept staring at me. This wasn't working.

I took a deep breath and started again.

"YOU," I said, pointing at her with both of my pointer fingers.

"ME," I said, pointing at myself.

"TRUNK," I said, reaching out and patting her trunk.

"UP," I said, pointing to the sky.

"OVER," I said, pointing to the fence.

Elsie just looked at me without moving.

"Give me a sign if you understand anything I just said,"

I begged her. "Please, Elsie."

Elsie shifted her weight as if she was getting ready to do something. I held my breath. Then a river of yellow water began pouring from her body making a puddle on the ground that grew into a lake that grew into an ocean.

I can tell you this. That wasn't the sign I was waiting for!

CHAPTER 7

Elsie looked down at the puddle, then raised her trunk and let out a happy trumpet.

"I understand," I said to her. "If I were you, I'd feel much better, too."

Elsie turned back to her lunch, pulling a giant clump of hay off the bale and shoving it into her mouth with her trunk. I knew that if I wanted to get her attention, it was going to have to involve hay. Here's a tip for you: You don't mess with an elephant when she's hungry.

I walked over to Elsie's lunch spot and grabbed a fistful of hay. No, I wasn't going to eat it. Like I said, I'm more of a hot dog guy. I held the hay out for Elsie to sniff. The tip of her long trunk nuzzled my hand—it actually felt like fingers tickling my palm. You'd be amazed how gentle such a huge animal can be. She took the hay and, curling her trunk toward her mouth, popped the whole handful in at once. I listened while she chewed. Then she burped.

"Well of course that's going to happen," I said. "You put too

much in your mouth at one time.
The same thing happens to me
when I'm sharing a pickle with
my grandfather, Papa Pete. I love
pickles so much, I shove the whole
thing in my mouth at once. Then
it's Burp City."

Elsie was more interested
in the hay than in my story. I
picked up another fistful and she
reached out for it with her trunk.
This time, I took a few steps
backward, and she followed me.
I took a few more steps toward
the fence that surrounded her
enclosure. She followed me again.
I kept repeating this until we were
almost touching the fence.

"That's a good girl," I said to

Elsie. "Now comes the hard part.
But I know you can do it. My mom
always says 'if you can imagine
it, you can make it happen.'
Of course, I don't know if that
applies to elephants, but I'm going
to be positive here and say that
it does."

I held the hay in front of me,
and Elsie stretched out her long
trunk. Instead of giving her the
hay, I took hold of her trunk with
my hands. Then she did the most
amazing thing. She curled up her
trunk so that it was in the shape
of a hook—the perfect place for
me to put my feet. I stepped onto
her trunk, wrapped my arms around
it, and held on tight.

"Now lift me up and put me down on the other side of the fence," I told her. "When I'm on the other side, you'll get your hay."

As Elsie lifted me high into the air, it felt like I was in an elevator with no walls. Trust me, you don't realize how tall an elephant is until you're riding on its trunk. I looked down at the ground. That was a bad idea. It was way down there. So instead, I looked straight ahead of me and tried to pretend that what was happening wasn't happening.

"Holy macaroni, Zip," I heard Frankie's voice call.

"Oh my goodness, what is going on?" Ms. Shimozato shouted.

"Elsie and I are working on a plan."

"Whatever it is, it looks extremely dangerous," she shouted.

"It sure does," Ashley agreed. "Hank, are you okay up there?"

"A little dizzy. I'm glad I didn't finish my scrambled eggs at breakfast, though. Did you guys find Nora?"

"We found someone who knew where she was and went to get her. We rushed back here to make sure you're okay," Ashley said.

"Zip!" Frankie called. "Can I just point out you're on an elephant trunk?"

I tried to sound calm, like riding an elephant's trunk was something I did every day. "Elsie is just giving me a little lift!"

"A little lift!" Ms. Shimozato cried. "You're scaring me, Hank!"

"Believe me, you're not the only one," I answered.

"Get down here right now!" Ms. Shimozato commanded.

"You heard him, Elsie," I said into her big ear. "Down, girl. Put me down on the other side of the fence."

Elsie stood very still for a minute, then her big eyes turned to look me right in the eye.

"You can do this," I told her. "One step forward and lower me down to my friends."

Elsie took a baby step forward. Let me remind you that a baby step for her is like a giant leap for us. Then she started to lower her trunk. Seventh floor. Sixth floor. Fifth floor. Soon, I was close enough to the ground to slide down her trunk like a firefighter coming down a firehouse pole. As my feet touched the ground, I put my hands in the air and shouted, "We did it! Thank you, Elsie!"

To my surprise, I heard what sounded like people clapping. I looked around, and for the first time, noticed that a group of people had gathered. They were all pointing at me. A few were even taking pictures.

"That's quite a show, kid," a man in a Yankees baseball cap called out.

"Do you do that every day at noon?" a woman holding a baby shouted.

"I really didn't do anything but hold on," I said to everyone. "Elsie did the hard part, didn't you, girl?" Elsie raised her trunk up to the sky and trumpeted loudly.

"That's right," I said to her. "You should be proud of yourself."

Elsie trumpeted again.

"Oh, I get it," I said. "You want your hay. Okay, here it is."

I held the hay out in my hand and Elsie's big trunk swooped down and picked it all up. Then the trunk and the hay disappeared over the fence.

"Hey everyone, I've got the key," Nora called, running down the path toward us. "What's the big emergency?"

"Hank was inside that enclosure with the elephant," Ms. Shimozato told her. "It was so frightening."

Nora turned to me. She looked shocked.

"You snuck in there?" she asked. "I hope you know that's very dangerous!"

"Not if you know Elsie like I do," I answered. "She's my friend. Did you know that she's a great soccer player?

"She's an elephant. Elephants don't play soccer."

Luckily, I didn't have to say a word. Elsie came to my rescue when a soccer ball came flying through the air. Usually I'm not very good at catching a ball, but this one was kicked up and over the fence, right to me. I reached out and grabbed it.

. The people who were gathered let out a huge cheer.

"That's amazing," the man
with the Yankees cap yelled.

"I want her on my team,"
a kid called out.

Nora turned to the elephant
enclosure. Elsie was standing at
the fence, waiting for me to kick
the ball back to her. I know it
seems weird, but I'd swear that
elephant was smiling.

CHAPTER 8

Nora couldn't believe her eyes.

"Did I just see what I think I saw?" she asked.

Frankie, Ashley, and I all nodded at the same time, as if we had planned it.

"You've seen her kick the ball like that before?" Nora asked me.

"Sure," I said. "Elsie and I have been playing a lot of soccer this morning."

Nora gave me a funny look.

"I'd like to see this with my own

eyes," Nora said. "Because since Elsie has been with us, she hasn't seemed at all playful. In fact, quite the opposite."

"Then just watch this," I said to her. I put the soccer ball on the ground.

"Okay, girl," I called out to Elsie. "Here it comes. Keep your eye on the ball."

Elsie flapped her ears, which was a good sign because it meant she was excited. I took aim and kicked the ball hard, while lifting my foot. The ball sailed over the fence and right to Elsie. As the ball rolled toward her, she put out her gigantic foot and just like that, kicked it back to me.

There was a gasp from the people in the crowd.

"Amazing," I heard Nora whisper.

We passed the ball back and forth again. When the ball was on my side of the fence, Elsie lifted her trunk and she trumpeted loudly, as if to say "She shoots, she scores!"

Nora actually started to laugh out loud.

"I don't know what you said to that elephant," she said to me, "but she sure is acting like a different animal."

"I think Elsie's ready to make new friends," I told Nora.

"We have to be careful putting

Elsie in with the others," she said. "Introducing a new elephant into a group can be risky. We have to be sure they all get along."

"But if you put Elsie in with the other elephants, they could start their own soccer team. Maybe I'll help you think of a name. My soccer team was the Sharks, but that would be a weird name for elephants. How about—"

Ms. Shimozato put her hand up to stop me.

"I hate to block your creativity, Hank," she said, "but I think you should leave the decisions about this elephant up to the zookeepers. I need to get you back to your class right away. I know Ms. Flowers is very worried. I would call her to let her know you're okay, but I left my phone at the snack bar."

"I'll let you go," Nora said. "Are you sure you know the way?"

Ms. Shimozato nodded and thanked Nora for her help. Then she led us up the path toward the snack bar.

"I hope Ms. Flowers hasn't called my parents," I said as we walked. "I'll be grounded until I'm old enough to shave."

"I've got to hand it to you, Zip," Frankie said with a laugh. "No matter how much trouble you're in, you're always funny."

We hurried up the red path, past the lions and the zebras.

"Oh look," I said, pointing to an especially beautiful zebra that was standing by the fence. "Can we just stop and try to count his stripes?"

"This is no time for stripe counting," Ms. Shimozato said.

"Okay, but I still think it was a good suggestion," I answered.

"I don't think you understand how much trouble you're in, Hank," Ashley whispered.

"Did you know that no two sets of zebra stripes are exactly alike?" I went on.

"Very interesting, Zip," Frankie said.

"Enough talking, kids," Ms. Shimozato said. "We've got to hurry."

Up ahead, at the end of the red trail, I saw the snack bar. Our whole class was sitting at the tables, looking bored. Ms. Flowers was on her phone, pacing back and forth. Nick McKelty was the first to notice us approaching.

"Well, it's about time, Zipper Teeth," he yelled out. "Our entire trip has been ruined because of you."

Ms. Flowers looked up from
her phone and immediately ran
toward us.

"Oh, thank goodness," she called out. "I've been so worried. Hank, are you okay?"

"He's fine," Ms. Shimozato said. "He was having an unusual encounter with an elephant."

"Wait until I tell you about it," I said.

"No, Hank! Now is not the time." Ms. Flowers sounded really angry. "I'm too upset. What was the first rule we discussed about our field trip?"

"Um . . . don't feed the animals?" I guessed.

"You see, this is an example of how you don't pay attention," Ms. Flowers scolded. "The most important rule we discussed was no wandering away. We specifically went over how everyone stays together, unless you are with your walking buddy."

I looked over at Nick, who was enjoying watching me get in all this trouble.

"My partner, whose name I won't say out loud but begins with an *N* and ends with an *elty,* ran off and left me in the bathroom."

"I did not!' McKelty yelled. "You were just too stupid to find me."

"That's enough, Nick," Ms. Flowers answered. "We don't call people names. I will handle this." Then turning to me, she said, "Hank, why didn't you return immediately?"

"That was my plan," I said truthfully. "But when I came out of the bathroom, I was lost. And then I saw Elsie and she seemed lonely, so I decided to stay with her awhile."

"Yeah," McKelty shouted. "And because of that, you're the only one who got to see the elephants. The rest of us had to sit here staring at our frozen lemonade cups."

I thought about what he said for a minute, and as much as I didn't want to admit it, Nick McKelty was right.

"I'm sorry," I said to everyone.

"I didn't mean to ruin the class trip. I guess I just wasn't thinking."

"Nothing new about that," McKelty grumbled.

Frankie put his hand on my shoulder.

"We know you didn't mean to mess things up," he whispered.

"Hank, I hope you understand that there will be consequences for what you did," Ms. Flowers said.

Here's one thing I have learned about adults. When they say, "There will be consequences," what they really mean is that you're going to get punished.

I looked at Ms. Flowers who was standing there with her arms folded in front of her. I gave her a little smile, but she did not smile back.

I knew what that meant.

Trouble with a capital *T*.

CHAPTER 9

FIVE POSSIBLE "CONSEQUENCES" THAT MIGHT HAPPEN

BY HANK ZIPZER

1. I will have to shovel up poop from the monkey habitat without the help of a nose clip.

2. I will have to sit next to Nick McKelty's armpits on all the class trips. Boy, I am really going to need that nose clip.

3. I will get the longest time-out in the history of the world. It will last so long that it will actually go into the Guinness Book of World Records.

4. I will have to write a three-paragraph report on my experience at the zoo. Three whole paragraphs! I'd rather shovel monkey poop!

5. I already forgot number five. So sorry, but that's life in the Zipzer brain.

CHAPTER 10

The good news was, I didn't
have to shovel up monkey poop.

The bad news was, I actually
got all of the other punishments,
plus some I had never thought of.

First of all, I had to sit next
to Nick McKelty on the bus ride
back to school. His armpits were
especially stinky after spending the
day at the zoo. My poor nose got
so tired from trying to block the
smell that I was going to have to
put it to bed early.

Second, when Ms. Flowers told my parents what I had done, I got grounded. My dad said for the next two weeks, I could eat, breathe, and go to school. And that was it.

Third, all of my screen time was taken away for two weeks. That meant no computer, no video games, and I couldn't even use my mom's phone to play a math game she had downloaded for me. When I tried to tell my dad that math was good for me, he said, "Use a pencil and paper instead." Then he put a whole sheet of subtraction problems in front of me. Was he kidding? I couldn't even do them behind me.

The hardest part of the punishment was writing the three-paragraph report on my experience at the zoo. For me, writing even one sentence is hard. Writing a paragraph is very, very hard. Writing three paragraphs is as close to impossible as a person can get.

After dinner that night, my dad set me up at the desk in my room. He gave me strict instructions.

"Don't come out of your room until you've written the three paragraphs," he said.

"But Dad," I answered. "This isn't fair. My brain is already cream cheese from working on those subtraction problems. Besides, I'm not a good paragraph writer."

"You should have thought of that before you wandered away, Hank. Now get to work. I want you in bed with the lights out at eight-thirty. And remember, don't get up from your desk until you finish the assignment."

As soon as my dad left the room, the first thing I did was get up from my desk. I had to.

My left leg was bouncing up and down like it had a motor in it. Or maybe it was my right leg. I have a hard time knowing my left from my right. But no matter what leg it was, I had to take it for a walk around my room.

I meant to go right back to my desk, but I made a little stop at my dresser and opened the drawer. The next thing I knew, I was looking through my collection of baseball cards. I don't know how they got out of order, but the Mets were all mixed together with the Yankees. I knew those cards wouldn't be happy until I separated them, because those two teams don't get along at all.

I took the cards out of my
drawer and put them down on the
carpet. I was busy sorting them
into two piles when the door
opened and my mom stuck her
head in.

"That doesn't look like writing
to me," she said, coming in and
closing the door behind her.

"You always say I have to get
organized," I answered. "Well,
look. I'm organizing."

"This is not going to help you get your report done," she pointed out. "You should be organizing your thoughts, not your baseball cards."

That was easy for her to say. When I tell my brain to organize my thoughts, it doesn't listen. It just thinks about whatever it wants to think about. And at that moment, it was thinking about baseball cards.

"Hank," my mom said. "This assignment shouldn't be hard for you. You know a lot about elephants. You've watched so many shows about them on television. Just combine what you already know with what you remember about your field trip. You'll be done in no time."

My mom helped me clean up the baseball cards and put them back in the drawer.

"The Yankees and the Mets are going to have to learn to get along on their own," I told her.

She laughed, but then put her hand on my shoulder like she does when she gets serious.

"Get to work, honey. Once your report is done, you'll feel so much better."

She left and I sat down at my desk, for real this time. I was determined to write my three paragraphs. I picked up one of the pencils and wrote my name at the top of the paper. Wow, that was a good start.

Then I thought of a title: "How to Hug an Elephant." I really liked that. I only had one problem. I couldn't spell *elephant*. Actually, I had two problems because I pushed so hard on the pencil, I snapped the point right off. It took me twenty minutes to find my pencil sharpener, which I finally found hidden under my rubber band collection. Once I was all set up with my sharpened pencil, the really hard part started. The thoughts were all there in my mind, waiting to come out. I just couldn't push them through my pencil. I'd write one word, then erase it. I erased over that spot so much, I erased a hole right through the paper. I thought it might help if I said the first two sentences out loud.

"Elsie is an elephant that has just moved to the zoo," I said to my empty room. "She weighs fifteen thousand pounds."

My ears loved those sentences!

Why couldn't I just get the words onto the paper in front of me?

I held the pencil and tried to write the first word. It didn't look right to me, probably because I spelled Elsie *L-z-y*. Then my mind took off on its own. I couldn't follow one thought. The facts of the television show got all mixed up with my visit to the zoo. Nothing made sense. My thoughts were out of order, just like my baseball cards.

I don't know how long I sat there trying to write the first sentence. It felt like twenty years, but I'm sure it was less. I was glad when my dad came in and told me it was eight-thirty.

I've never wanted to go to bed so much in my whole life.

"Did you do a good job?" my dad asked as I put the page with only the title and my name on it into my backpack.

"Dad, I did the best job I could."

It wasn't really a lie. I had tried. And tried. And tried.

"I hope you learned your lesson," was all he said. "Now go to bed."

I put on my pajamas and walked down the hall to the bathroom. As I brushed my teeth, I stared at myself in the mirror. I tried to imagine how I was going to explain to

Ms. Flowers that all I had for her was an empty page with a hole in it. But the only thing I saw was a worried kid with a mouthful of toothpaste and not even one paragraph to turn in.

CHAPTER 11

It took me a long time to walk to school the next morning. It was the same distance as always— a half block to the corner and another half block to PS 87. But I was walking as slowly as I could because I knew what was waiting for me when I got there.

"You're walking as slow as a snail this morning," Frankie noticed.

"Actually," my sister, Emily, chimed in. "Snails don't walk.

Walking means you have legs. Snails glide on surfaces."

"Fine," Frankie said. "Then Hank is gliding very slowly on the sidewalk surface."

Frankie's mom, who was taking us to school, agreed.

"Usually you're bouncing all around, Hank," she said. "Like yesterday, when you apparently didn't stay with your class during the field trip."

"You know about that, too?" I asked.

"Sure," she said. "We discussed your elephant adventure over our meatloaf and mashed potatoes last night."

"My family discussed it over

chocolate pudding," Ashley said.

Was the whole world talking about my mistake? I guess they were. And the worst part was, so was Principal Love. I found that out the minute I arrived at school.

He was standing on the front steps in his weird Velcro sneakers, greeting all the students. As soon as he saw me, he came marching over. I could hear his sneakers squeaking on the pavement. I didn't like the sound of that.

"Well, young man, that was quite a scare you gave everyone yesterday."

I noticed that the mole on his cheek, which looks like the Statue of Liberty, seemed to be shaking its head at me. Was his mole angry, too?

"Ms. Flowers said that part of your punishment was to write a report on your trip to the zoo," he went on. "I'll be there for your presentation."

"You mean you're coming to my class?"

"Yes, indeed."

"And actually sitting down to listen to me?"

"Yes, indeed, again."

"Wow," I said. "That's going to be so . . . um . . . it's going to be so . . . I just can't think of the word right now."

"There are many words to describe my visit," Principal Love said. "Thrilling. Stimulating. Delightful."

I didn't tell him, but, actually, the word I had in mind was *scary*. Really scary.

CHAPTER 12

I kept hoping that Ms. Flowers had forgotten about my three-paragraph report. She didn't mention it after she took attendance. She didn't mention it when she wrote her quote of the day on the board. She didn't mention it when she announced that it was taco day in the cafeteria. I was starting to feel pretty good and was even thinking how much I'd like a taco for lunch.

But then Principal Love

walked in, and I lost my appetite completely.

"Principal Love has joined us for Hank's presentation," Ms. Flowers said to the class. "Hank, are you ready?"

My mind screamed no. My mouth said yes.

"Fine," she said. "Please come up to the front of the class and read us your report."

I opened my notebook and took out the piece of lined paper I had worked on. Nick McKelty leaned across his desk as far as he could without flipping over. Even though I tried to hide the paper, he got a quick look at it.

"Hey, there's nothing written on

there," he shouted. "It's totally empty."

"It is not," I said. "See, there's the title, *How to Hug an Elephant.*"

"Oh is that what it says?" McKelty snorted. "To me, it looks like somebody threw up on your paper."

"Nick, that's enough," Ms. Flowers said. "Hank, can I please see your report?"

My heart started to beat faster.

"It's not what it looks like," I said as I got close to her desk. "I know it looks empty, but there's a lot of thought behind it."

Ms. Flowers held out her hand, and I had no choice but to give her the paper.

"Hank," she said, looking at both sides. "There's nothing but a big hole in the middle of this page."

"I know. That's where all the thoughts fell through. They went right down that hole and into the carpet in my bedroom. But luckily for all of us, I still have them here in my mind."

Before she could answer, I turned to the class and started to talk.

"Yesterday I had the most amazing experience with Elsie the

elephant," I began. "I learned that Elsie can use the end of her trunk like fingers. That's how she picks up things to eat. I also learned that if an elephant raises her trunk up in the air while she's trumpeting, it means she's happy to see you. But the most important thing I learned from Elsie is that elephants have feelings as big as their bodies."

"How'd you learn that?" McKelty shouted out. "Did you two dance or something?"

"Actually, Elsie and I played soccer. And it turns out she's a natural. She could score a goal from a mile away."

"I don't believe you," he said.

"Well, it's true. You can ask

Frankie and Ashley. They saw her do it."

"We sure did," Frankie said.

"That Elsie's got a great goal kick," Ashley added.

"Elephants are the largest land animals in the world," I continued. "When one of their friends in the herd dies, they feel sad. When Elsie arrived at the zoo, she felt very sad. But after my visit with her, I believe she showed the zookeeper another side of her, a happy side."

"Sounds like you helped her feel better, Hank," Katie Sperling said. "I think that's so cool."

A bunch of the other kids nodded.

"Yeah, I think I did. So I'm really sorry that I scared everyone by getting lost. And that I did something dangerous by going into the enclosure. I'm also sorry I messed up your visit to the zoo. But I hope you understand that something wonderful happened with Elsie."

"I have a question," Principal Love said from the back of the room.

"Okay, Principal Love. I call on you."

"Your behavior prevented your classmates from enjoying the field trip as much as you did," he said. "How do you plan to make that up to them?"

That was a good question. I had been thinking about it a lot.

"First, let me repeat to everyone how sorry I am. And second, I have decided to donate everything in my piggy bank to a Save the Elephants organization. Elephants like Elsie are in danger, and I want to help them."

"Why, Hank, what a wonderful idea," Ms. Flowers said.

"I counted my money last night, and I'm pretty sure I have twenty-seven dollars and thirteen cents. It might be fifteen cents, I just couldn't keep track. Anyway, I'm donating the money in the name of all of you in Ms. Flowers's second-grade class."

To my surprise, everyone started to cheer.

"I think you should give the money to us," Nick McKelty blurted out.

Everyone started to boo. That felt amazing. Even though I had ruined their field trip, they were sticking up for me. Well, actually not for me, but for Elsie and all the other elephants in the world.

"I'm glad to see that you've learned your lesson," Principal Love said. "And on top of that, you've taught us all an important one. I'm sure that Elsie and her elephant friends will benefit from your kindness. Well done, young man."

My ears couldn't believe that Principal Love was talking about me.

I stood there in front of my class.

And you know what? I felt proud. My trip to the zoo turned out to be the greatest field trip ever.

CHAPTER 13

SIX INCREDIBLE FACTS ABOUT ELEPHANTS

BY HANK ZIPZER

1. Elephants can live to be over seventy years old. Wow, that's even older than Papa Pete!

2. An elephant's skin is an inch thick. So is my sister's head.

3. Elephants purr like cats. It must be really hard when they try to curl up in your lap.

4. An elephant tooth can weigh five pounds and is as big as a brick. I wonder where they sell toothbrushes that big.

5. Elephants sometimes "hug" by wrapping their trunks together. Just the thought of that makes me happy.

6. Elephants are in danger from people who want to kill them for their ivory tusks. If you want to help them as much as I do, you can learn all about elephants at websites for groups like the World Wildlife Organization (www.worldwildlife.org) or United for Wildlife (unitedforwildlife.org).